Librarian Reviewer
Laurie K. Holland
Media Specialist (National Board Certified), Edina, MN
MA in Elementary Education, Minnesota State University, Mankato

Reading Consultant
Mark DeYoung
Classroom Teacher, Edina Public Schools, MN
BA in Elementary Education, Central College
MS in Curriculum & Instruction, University of MN

Graphic Sparks are published by Stone Arch Books,
A Capstone Imprint
1710 Roe Crest Drive
North Mankato, Minnesota 56003
www.capstonepub.com

Library of Congress Cataloging-in-Publication Data
Hoena, B. A.
    Eek and Ack, Invaders from the Great Goo Galaxy / by Blake A Hoena; illustrated
by Steve Harpster.
    p. cm. — (Graphic Sparks. Eek and Ack)
    ISBN-13: 978-1-59889-052-5 (library binding)
    ISBN-10: 1-59889-052-2 (library binding)
    ISBN-13: 978-1-59889-225-3 (paperback)
    ISBN-10: 1-59889-225-8 (paperback)
    1. Graphic novels. I. Harpster, Steve. II. Title. III. Series.
PN6727.H57I58 2007
741.5'973—dc22   2006007697

Summary: Eek and Ack, two alien brothers from another galaxy, are egged on by their older sister, Bleck, to conquer Earth. When they arrive in a spaceship that looks like a washing machine, they get into some sudsy trouble.

Art Director: Heather Kindseth
Cover Graphic Designer: Heather Kindseth
Interior Graphic Designer: Keegan Gilbert

EEK & ACK

INVADERS

FROM THE GREAT GOO GALAXY

BY BLAKE A. HOENA

ILLUSTRATED BY STEVE HARPSTER

CAST OF CHARACTERS

Bleck - Eek and Ack's older sister

Eek - space alien kid

Mom - Eek and Ack's mother

Ack - Eek's brother, slightly younger by a few hundred years

9

12

14

ABOUT THE AUTHOR

Blake A. Hoena spends his nights holding a laundry basket of dirty clothes and staring up at the stars. He doesn't know if there really are aliens, but he wants to be ready just in case Eek and Ack return to Earth. This is the first book he's written about aliens. Usually he writes about dogs, pigs, sheep, and camels.

ABOUT THE ILLUSTRATOR

Steve Harpster has loved to draw funny cartoons, mean monsters, and goofy gadgets since he was able to pick up a pencil. In first grade, he was able to avoid his writing assignments by working on the pictures for stories instead. Steve was able to land a job drawing funny pictures for books, and that's really what he's best at. Steve lives in Columbus, Ohio, with his wonderful wife, Karen, and their sheepdog, Doodle.

GLOSSARY

conquest (KON-kwest)—to defeat and take control of something

hover (HUHV-ur)—to remain in one place while flying, which is the right way to use a rocket pack when playing indoors

kabobbler (ka-BOB-lur)—any tool used to fix a spaceship; a de-fizzler also works

Milky Way (MILK-ee WAY)—the galaxy that includes Earth, our entire solar system, and about 100 billion stars!

vaporize (VAY-pur-eyez)—to turn anything solid into smoke, mist or steam; usually done with a vaporizer, an alien's favorite invention

whizzler speed (WHIZ-lur speed)—faster than twizzler speed but slower than swizzler speed. Whizzler is the normal speed for a washing machine flying through space.

EEK AND ACK'S GALAXY OF FACTS

My brothers think they know everything.

Did you know that a blue moon isn't really blue? "Blue moon" is the name for the second full moon that shows up in a month. This only happens every two and a half to three years. That's why, when something rare happens, we say it happens "once in a blue moon."

Scientists know more about outer space than they *do about* our deepest oceans.

One day on the Pluto is the same amount of time as a week here on Earth. Wow, and you thought the school day lasted forever!

We do!

If you shouted in space, even someone standing right next to you couldn't hear you. Sound doesn't travel in space. Aliens have all the luck!

Think you want to count all the stars in the galaxy? If you counted one star each second, it would take you three thousand years. Hmm, should have started sooner!

If you were driving 75 miles per hour, it would take you about 258 days to circle one of Saturn's rings.

What foot did Neil Armstrong use to step onto the moon? His left.

DISCUSSION QUESTIONS

1. Eek and Ack have very different personalities. How do they react differently to situations in the story? Use an event in the story to explain your answer.

2. Eek is happy to be working on his spaceship, until his sister Bleck shows up. Why does Eek's attitude change around his older sister?

3. Eek and Ack's spaceship looks like a washing machine, and they crash land outside a laundromat. Do you think the author planned this from the start? How would the story be different if Eek and Ack landed somewhere else, for instance, such as an animal shelter or a bowling alley?

WRITING PROMPTS

1. Hurry, hurry! A UFO has just landed in your backyard! Describe what the ship looks like, if the aliens are friendly, and why they have come to Earth. If it helps, draw a picture first.

2. Imagine you lived on a faraway planet. Describe how things would be different because of your alien home. What would school be like, what type of pets would you have, how would you play your favorite sports? Describe your life.

3. What if Eek and Ack succeeded in conquering Earth? What would things be like on our planet if two alien kids ran things? Write about it!